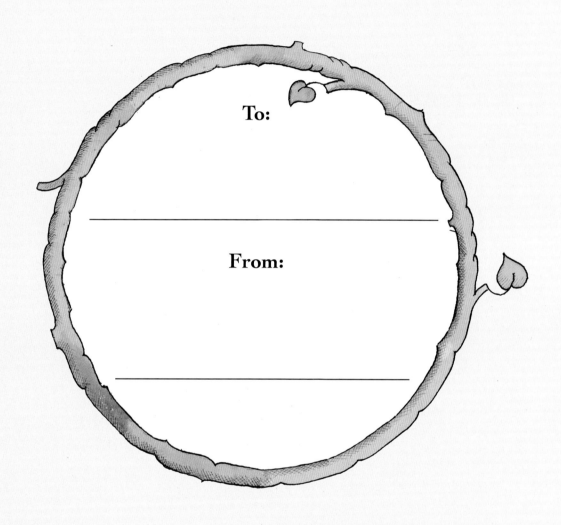

To:

_____

From:

_____

Based on the NBC animated special *The Berenstain Bears Meet Bigpaw*

Copyright © 2022 Berenstain Publishing, Inc. All rights reserved. Published in the United States by Random House Children's Books, a division of Penguin Random House LLC, New York. Random House and the colophon are registered trademarks of Penguin Random House LLC.

Visit us on the Web!
rhcbooks.com
BerenstainBears.com

Educators and librarians, for a variety of teaching tools, visit us at RHTeachersLibrarians.com

Library of Congress Control Number: 2021950724
ISBN 978-0-593-48282-7 (trade) — ISBN 978-0-593-48461-6 (ebook)

MANUFACTURED IN CHINA
10 9 8 7 6 5 4 3 2 1

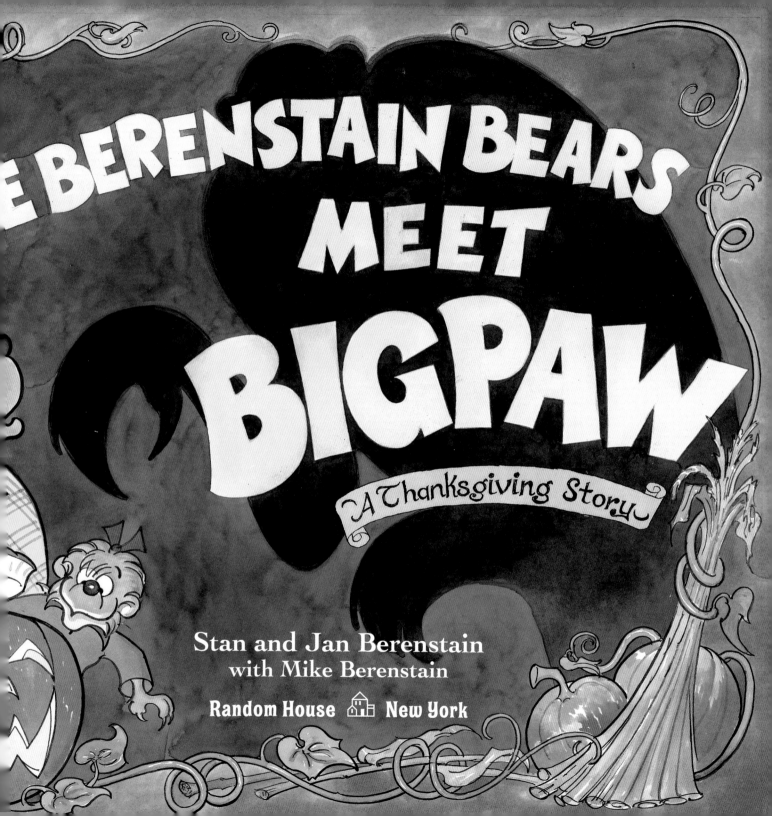

E BERENSTAIN BEARS MEET BIGPAW

A Thanksgiving Story

Stan and Jan Berenstain
with Mike Berenstain

Random House 🏠 New York

MAMA

Beauty Is as Beauty Does

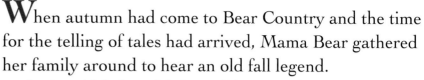hen autumn had come to Bear Country and the time for the telling of tales had arrived, Mama Bear gathered her family around to hear an old fall legend.

"It is said," she told them, "that one day, when Thanksgiving time draws near, a great danger may threaten Bear Country."

"What danger, Mama?" asked Sister.

"The danger of Bigpaw!" replied Mama.

"Bigpaw?" wondered the cubs. "What's that?"

"The legend tells us," said Mama, "that if we grow lazy and greedy and fail to share nature's great bounty with those in need, then Bigpaw—that monster of monsters—will come stomping out of the swamp and gobble up all of Bear Country, county by county!"

Sister and Brother shivered. But Papa just laughed.

"Stuff and nonsense!" he chuckled. "Nonsense and stuff! There's no such thing as Bigpaw!"

"We shall see what we shall see," replied Mama.

"What I see," said Papa, "is a beautiful fall day. Halloween is almost here, and Thanksgiving right after. Let's get ready for the holidays—let's enjoy the beautiful fall weather."

Then they marched out to celebrate all things autumn! They carved a pumpkin for Halloween and sang a song to the spirit of Thanksgiving.

PAPA

A Bear for All Seasons

"We're thankful for our family—
for trusted friends, for home sweet tree.
We're thankful, which is why we stress
thankful, thankful, thankfulness!
Yes! Yes! Yes! Yes, we stress
thankful, thankful, thankfulness!"

"I am thankful for Thanksgiving dinner!" said Papa Bear. "There'll be sweet potatoes and stuffing; two kinds of pie; mashed potatoes and gravy; turkey, of course; cranberry sauce; corn on the cob . . . and, oh yes, my favorite treat—"

"We know," said Brother and Sister. "Mixed nuts!"

"Say," whispered Sister to Brother. "Let's pick some mixed nuts to give to Papa as a treat on Thanksgiving!"

"Yes," agreed Brother. "They grow on the mixed-nut tree down in Sinister Bog. Let's go!"

BROTHER
&
SISTER

Cubs, Loyal and True

Meanwhile, in the depths of Sinister Bog, something was happening. The swamp critters could sense it. The ground was trembling. Something big was stomping its way nearer and nearer. Frogs and turtles hid in the reeds. Swamp birds tucked their heads under their wings. Even the swamp crocs hunkered down low in the water, pretending they were floating logs. What was coming their way?

It was Bigpaw, of course!

He had arms like tree trunks, shoulders like boulders, and a nose like a turnip!

Was the Thanksgiving legend finally coming true?

Nearby, Brother and Sister
arrived at the mixed-nut tree.
They climbed the tree and
started to gather nuts.

Then, suddenly, the branches
began to sway—and the cubs fell
out of the tree!

Thankfully, a giant hand reached out to catch them. It was the huge hand of Bigpaw himself! To the cubs' surprise, Bigpaw placed them gently on the ground.

They realized Bigpaw wasn't a gentle giant!

"Thank you for saving us, Mr. Bigpaw!" said the cubs.

"Uh . . . you're welcome!" Bigpaw replied shyly.

The cubs knew they had to tell everyone in Bear Country that Bigpaw was no monster. He was just a very, very BIG bear!

When the cubs told Papa about Bigpaw, he wasn't so sure. What if Bigpaw was a dangerous stranger after all?

The cubs convinced Papa to meet Bigpaw and see for himself. So the cubs led him up the mountain, to the spot where Bigpaw was settling down for the night. But in the firelight, Bigpaw's huge shadow did look like a terrible monster. Papa was terrified!

"Oh no!" he cried. "Bigpaw is coming! We must prepare to meet the stranger!"

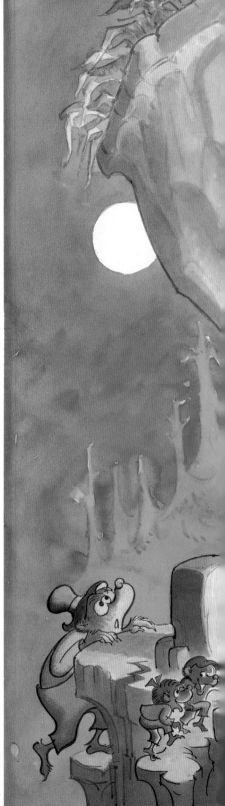

Papa sounded the alarm. The townsfolk raced out to defend Bear Country.

"Now, hold on," said Mama. "Let's not get carried away. This stranger doesn't sound dangerous. After all, what is a stranger?"

"What do you mean, Mama?" asked the cubs.

"Let me explain . . . ," said Mama.

"A stranger's just somebody
you don't already know.
He could be a friend.
He could be a foe,
or just a regular sort of a Joe.
So try not to forget—
a stranger's just somebody
you haven't yet met!"

But Papa was not convinced. He was ready to defend Bear Country from the great Bigpaw menace.

"Oh no! Not that old cannon. It's sure to blow up!" warned Mama.

"Don't worry," replied Papa. "We're going to test it first."

Papa dusted himself off and led the townsfolk up the mountain toward Bigpaw.

"Forward!" he called.

The cubs tried to stop Papa and talk sense to their neighbors, but no one would listen!

Instead, they ran ahead to warn Bigpaw. But Bigpaw was ready to defend himself from the attacking bears with a big pile of boulders!

"Wait!" cried Brother and Sister as they stood between the bears and Bigpaw.

When Papa and the townsfolk spotted the cubs, they thought Brother and Sister were in danger! What if those teetering boulders should fall? Just then, Bigpaw reached down and safely scooped up the cubs!

The bears let out a gasp. Bigpaw really was a gentle giant after all.

"Hooray for Bigpaw!" yelled Papa.

"Hooray!" everyone cheered.

When Thanksgiving Day arrived, the Bear family was truly thankful.

"I am thankful that we have learned to share our bounty with our fellow bear," said Papa.

"Uh . . . excuse me," interrupted Bigpaw as he ducked into the room. "But you cubs left this behind."

"Mixed nuts!" exclaimed Papa. "Why, thank you, Bigpaw!"

"We are thankful, too," said the cubs. "We are thankful for our wonderful new friend, Bigpaw Bear!"

"Awww, thank you!" said Bigpaw shyly.